WAY TO BE!

How to Be Brave, Responsible, Honest, and an All-Around Great Kid

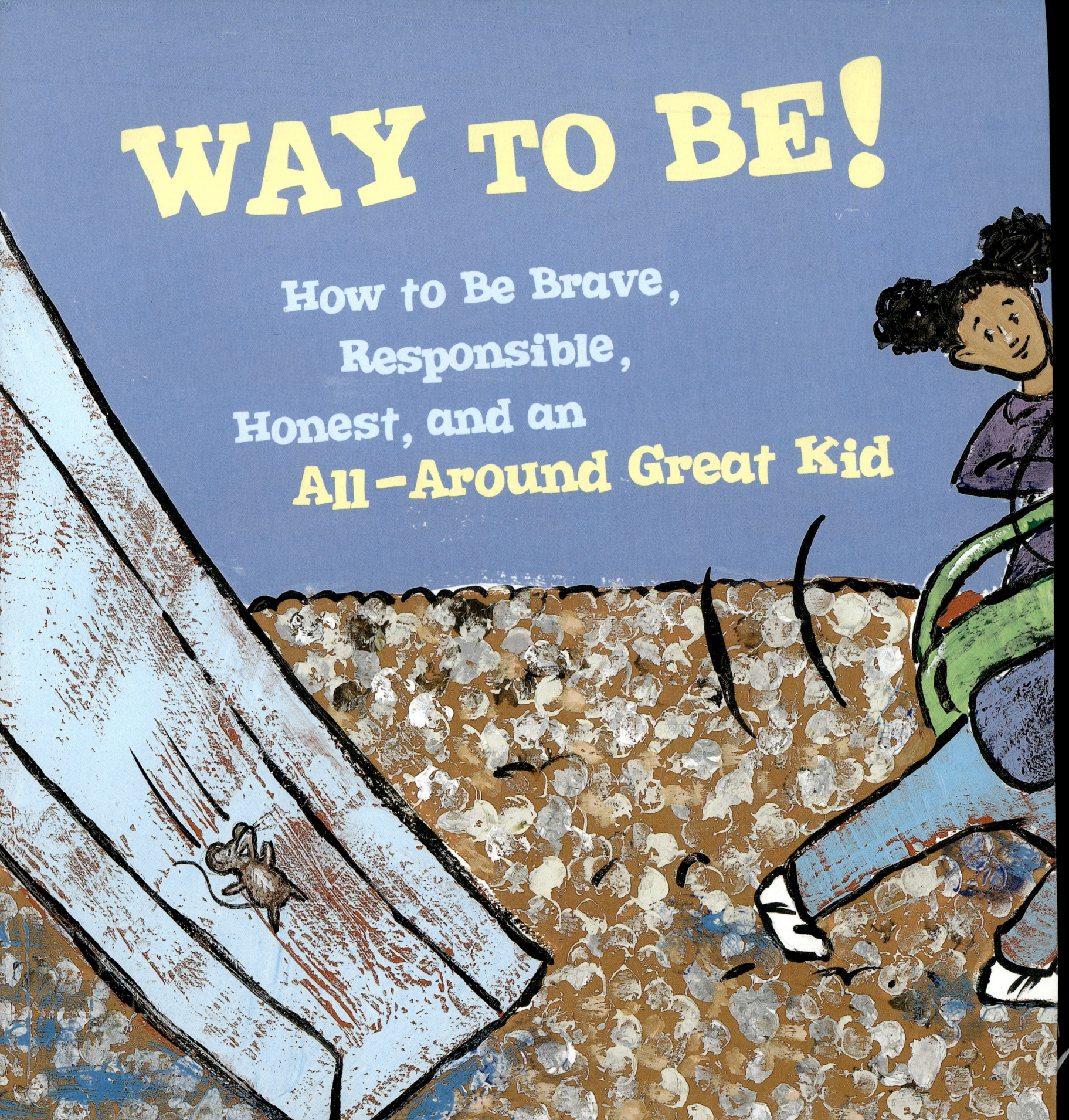

WAY TO BE!

How to Be Brave, Responsible, Honest, and an All-Around Great Kid

by Jill Lynn Donahue and Mary Small
illustrated by Stacey Previn

Table of Contents

Being Brave 6

Being Considerate 18

Being Cooperative 30

Being Fair 42

Being a Good Citizen 54

Being Honest 66

Being Respectful 78

Being Responsible 90

Being Tolerant 102

Being Trustworthy 114

Being Brave

Being brave means facing your fears. Brave people do the right thing, even when it is not easy. Brave people may feel afraid sometimes. But they do what needs to be done. There are many ways to be brave.

The doctor says Alexa needs two shots. Alexa doesn't like shots, but she knows they will keep her healthy.

Alexa is being brave.

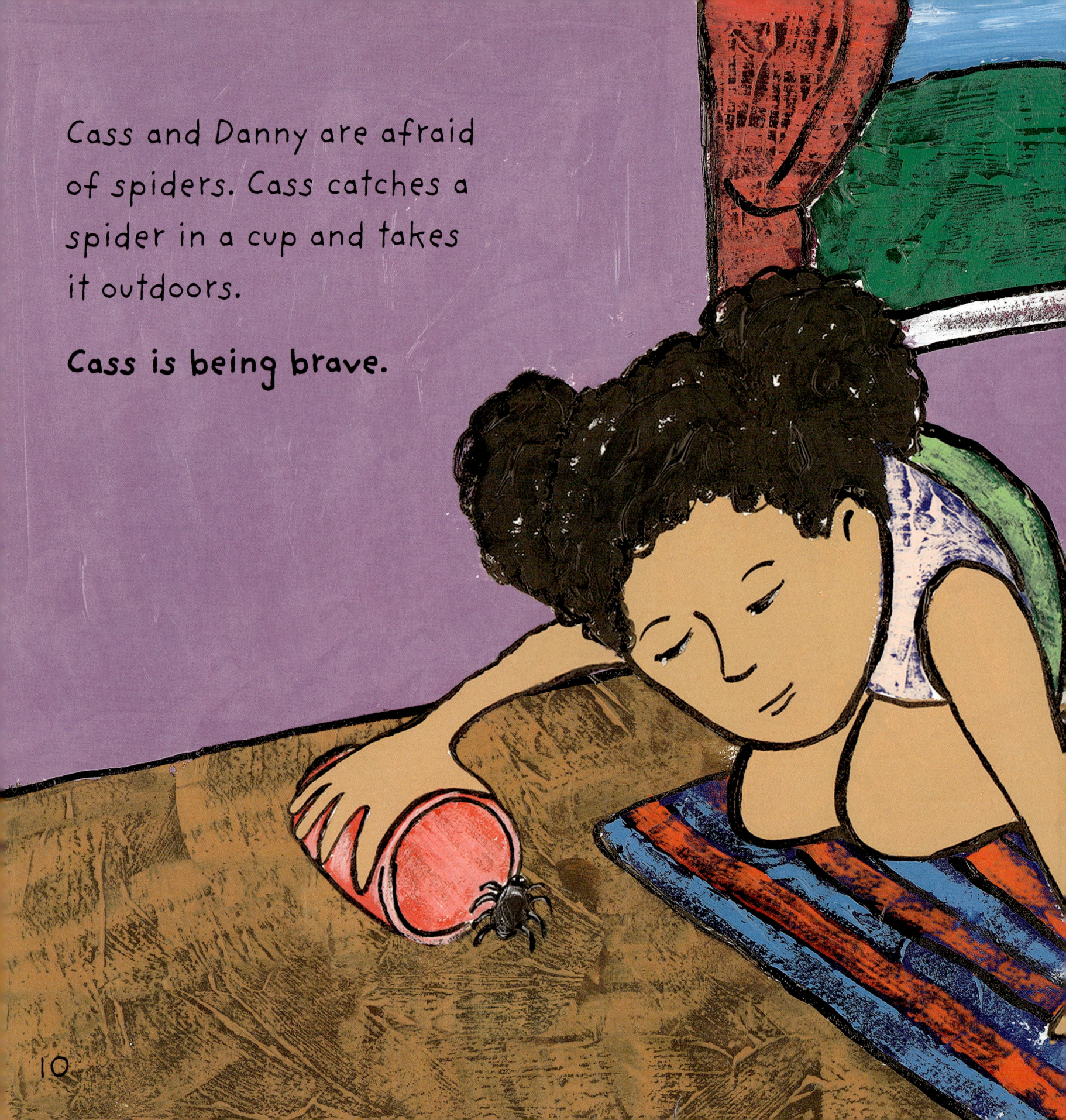

Cass and Danny are afraid of spiders. Cass catches a spider in a cup and takes it outdoors.

Cass is being brave.

Eddie's friends think it is cool to take off their hats while waiting for the bus. Eddie knows his friends might tease him, but he leaves his hat on.

Eddie is being brave.

Tim is worried about his first trip on an airplane. But he holds his mom's hand and gets on the plane.

Tim is being brave.

Enrico doesn't like talking in front of his class. He takes a deep breath and tells a funny story.

Enrico is being brave.

Being Considerate

Being considerate means caring for other people, thinking about their feelings, and trying to help them. Considerate people are respectful and use good manners. There are many ways to be considerate.

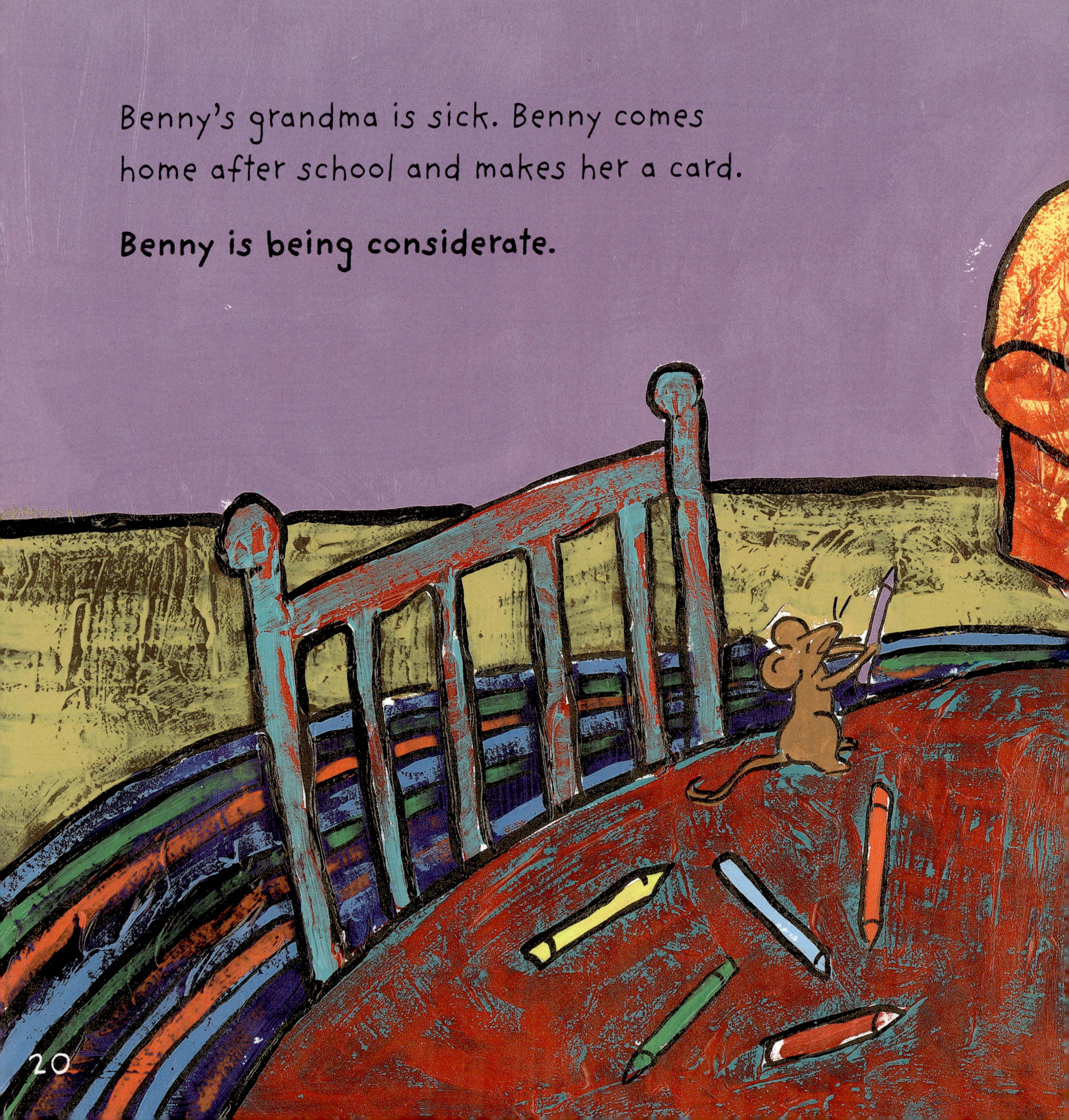

Benny's grandma is sick. Benny comes home after school and makes her a card.

Benny is being considerate.

While the neighbors are away on vacation, Roland waters their flowers.

Roland is being considerate.

Sonya's bike is older than Violet's. When they ride together, Violet rides slowly and waits for Sonya.

Violet is being considerate.

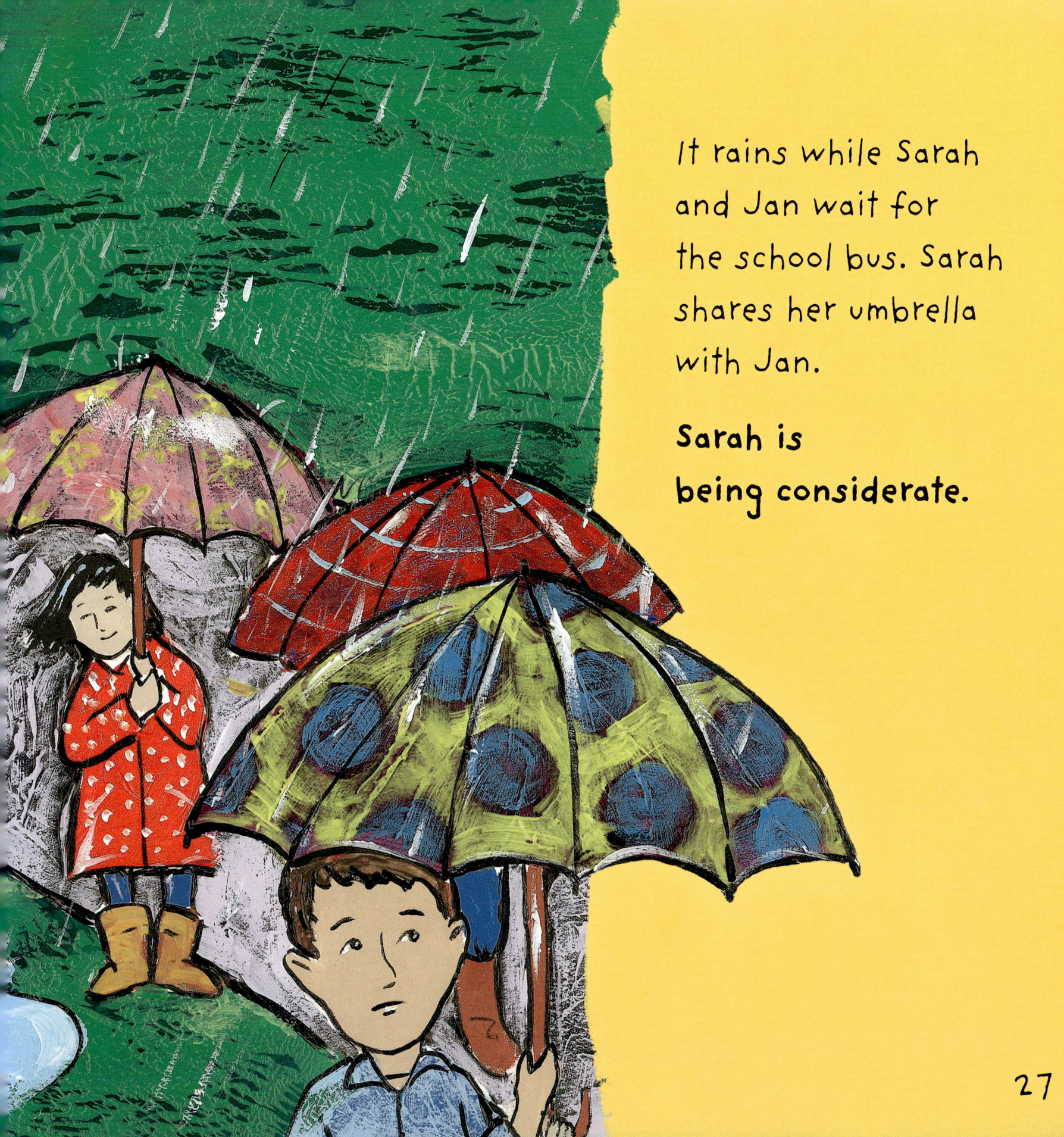

It rains while Sarah and Jan wait for the school bus. Sarah shares her umbrella with Jan.

Sarah is being considerate.

Madison and her family camp at a state park. They clean up after themselves before they go home.

Madison and her family are being considerate.

Being Cooperative

Being cooperative means working with others as a group. People who work together can often get things done better and faster than someone who works alone. Cooperative people know that by doing their part, everyone is better off.

There are many leaves in Maya's yard. Maya's family members work together to rake up the leaves.

Maya's family members are being cooperative.

Max is trying to build a big snow fort. Max's friends add snowballs so they can all hide behind the fort.

Max and his friends are being cooperative.

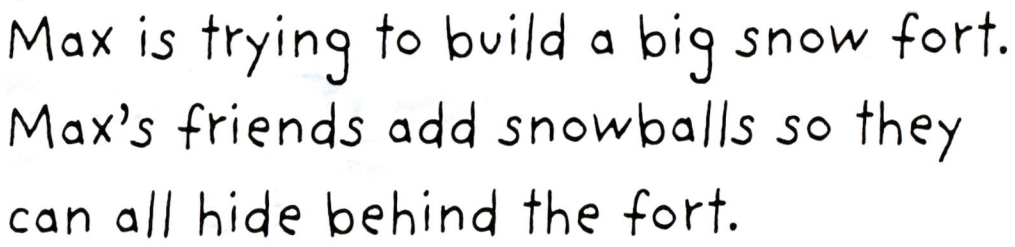

At recess, seven friends want to ride the merry-go-round. The friends all take turns pushing.

The friends are being cooperative.

Layla and her friends find a big branch on the bike trail. They all help pull the branch off the trail.

Layla and her friends are being cooperative.

Four friends want to have a lemonade stand. Each one of them brings something they will need.

The friends are being cooperative.

40.

Being Fair

Being fair means that you treat other people the way you want to be treated. This is called the Golden Rule. We can follow the Golden Rule and show fairness even to strangers and people we just met. There are many ways to be fair.

Erin lets an older woman have her seat on the bus so the woman doesn't have to stand.

Erin is being fair.

Jared helps his dad do chores around the house before going to play with his friends.

Jared is being fair.

Before anyone else gets blamed, Julie admits that she broke the cookie jar.

Julie is being fair.

The kids make sure everyone gets to join in the fun.

They are being fair.

Being a Good Citizen

Living in a country is like being part of a big, special club. You are a member of that club every day. If your club is going to be a success, every member has to help. Being a good citizen means you are helping your country be the best it can be. There are many ways to be a good citizen.

Joe knows the lakes need to be cleaner, so he speaks out against pollution.

Joe is being a good citizen.

Kelly helps shovel her neighbor's sidewalk after it snows.

Kelly is being a good citizen.

Stacy picks up the trash from the ground and throws it away even though it is not hers.

Stacy is being a good citizen.

Jenna works as a crossing guard to help keep people and animals safe.

Jenna is being a good citizen.

Josh protects the small and weak from harm.

Josh is being a good citizen.

Being Honest

Being honest means telling the truth. Even though it may sometimes be hard, telling the truth is the right thing to do. Honest people do not tell lies, cheat, or steal. Honest people can be trusted.

Tanya's neighbor pays Tanya too much money for feeding the cat. Tanya returns the extra money.

Tanya is being honest.

Andy finds a purse on his way to school. He takes nothing from the purse. When he gets to school, he gives it to his teacher.

Andy is being honest.

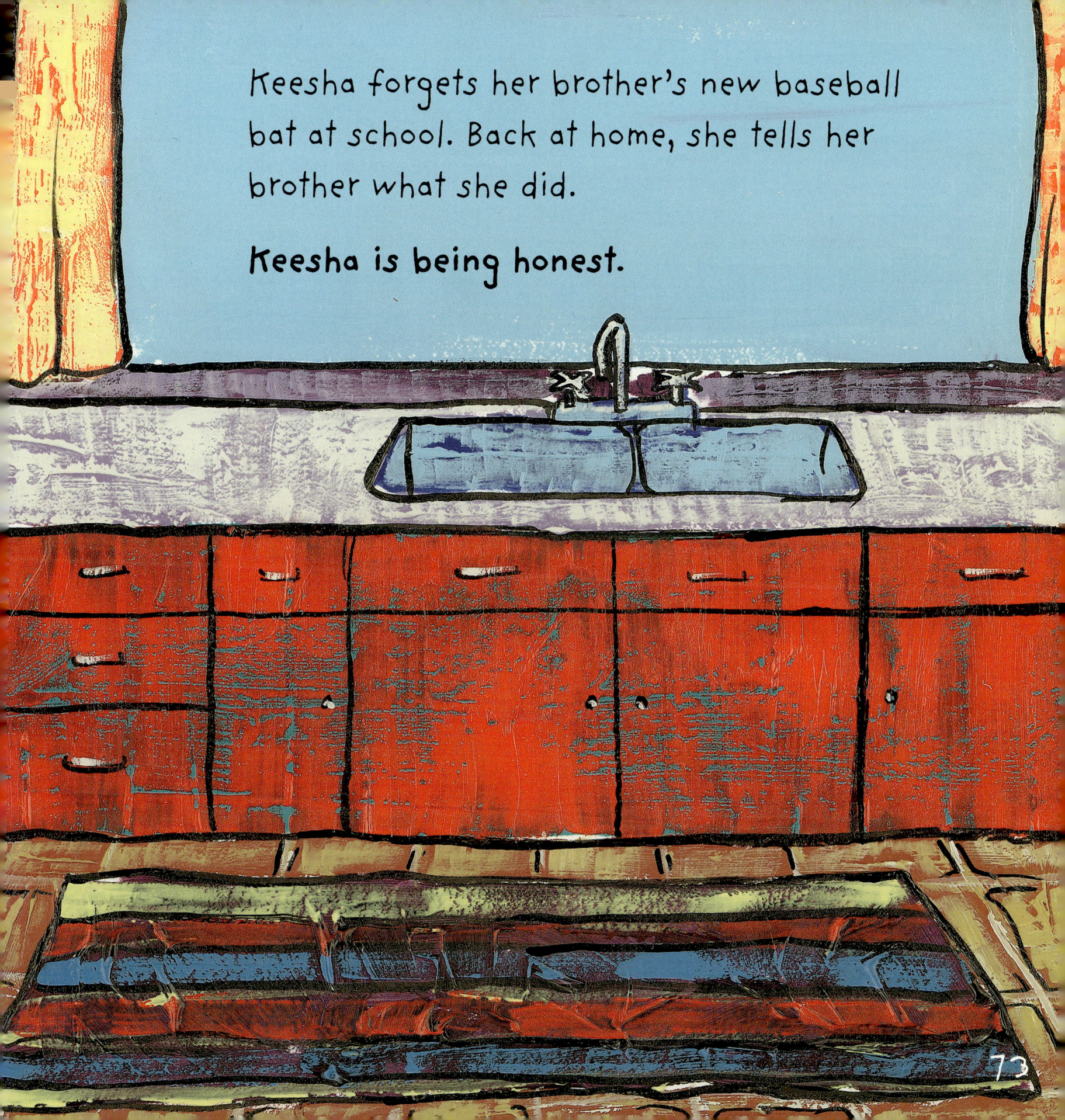

Keesha forgets her brother's new baseball bat at school. Back at home, she tells her brother what she did.

Keesha is being honest.

Being Respectful

Showing respect means caring how a person feels. Showing respect means doing things that show another person you think they are important. There are lots of ways to show respect.

Christine's uncle is allergic to cats. When he visits she takes Muffy out of the room.

Christine is showing respect.

While playing in the yard, Mike is careful not to step on the flowers.

Mike is showing respect.

Joe takes care of himself. He bathes, studies, eats healthy foods, and gets plenty of rest

Joe is showing respect for himself.

Being Responsible

Being responsible means doing the things you are supposed to do. No one else can do your homework or chores for you. No one else can tell the truth for you. These are things only you can do by yourself. When you do what you are supposed to do, you are being responsible. There are lots of ways to show you are responsible.

Patricia cleans up after her dog when they are taking a walk or playing in the park.

Patricia is being responsible.

Kelly and her brothers rush to get ready.
They want to catch the bus on time.

They are being responsible.

Bridget wears a helmet when riding her bike.

Bridget is being responsible.

Zach feeds his animals on time.

Zach is being responsible.

Jamie returns her library books on time.

Jamie is being responsible.

Being Tolerant

Being tolerant means being respectful of the differences among people. Tolerant people can be friends with people who are very different from themselves. There are many ways to be tolerant.

Gunnar's friends ask him to play a word game. Gunnar is slow at first, but his friends are patient.

Gunnar's friends are being tolerant.

Maria and Betsy form a club for girls only. Later Tim asks if he can join their club. The girls change the rules so Tim can join the club.

The girls are being tolerant.

Miguel's family celebrates Christmas. John's family celebrates Hanukkah. Their families join each other for both of the holidays.

The families are being tolerant.

Tyson has to get glasses. The next day none of his classmates make fun of his new glasses.

The students are being tolerant.

Stan's parents like the mayor. Michael's parents want a new mayor. Stan's and Michael's families are friends.

The families are being tolerant.

Being Trustworthy

Being trustworthy sometimes takes courage. It isn't always easy. But it is worth the work to have people trust you. There are lots of ways to show you are trustworthy.

In school the students are sure to keep their eyes on their own test.

They are being trustworthy.

Jeremy takes the trash out when it is his turn. His parents can rely on him.

Jeremy is being trustworthy.

Greg goes to the store for his dad. He gives his dad all of the change.

Greg is being trustworthy.

Paul points out to Mrs. Baker that money fell out of her purse.

Paul is being trustworthy.

Candace comes home exactly when she said she'd be there.

Candace is being trustworthy.

About the Authors

Jill Donahue has worked as a newspaper carrier, burger flipper, jewelry salesperson, industrial safety officer, chemist, editor, and writer—in that order! She has written many children's books. She is a true-blue Wisconsin woman who loves community volunteering, reading, motorcycling, boating, taking long walks around lakes, and Friday-night fish fries. Jill lives in central Wisconsin with her daughter, son, husband, and two cats.

Mary Small is a freelance writer who helps leaders of health care organizations communicate with their employees, patients, and communities. She is the author of several children's books and many magazine articles about medicine and health. Her writing reflects her experience with all kinds of people—all ages, backgrounds, religions, and nationalities. Mary lives in Minnesota and is the mother of a grown son.

About the Illustrator

Stacey Previn has been an illustrator for more than 20 years and has worked on many children's books. She lives in Oak Park, Illinois, with her husband, two sons, and two mischievous hamsters. She has also done extensive advertising and editorial work for well-known companies.

Editor: Shelly Lyons
Designers: Tracy Davies and Eric Manske
Art Director: Nathan Gassman
The illustrations in this book were created with acrylics.
Picture Window Books
151 Good Counsel Drive
Box 669
Mankato, MN 56002-0669
877-845-8392
www.capstonepub.com

Copyright © 2011 by Picture Window Books,
a Capstone imprint.
All rights reserved. No part of this book may be reproduced
without written permission from the publisher. The publisher
takes no responsibility for the use of any of the materials or
methods described in this book, nor for the products thereof.
Printed in the United States of America
in Stevens Point, Wisconsin.
082010
005906R

All books published by Picture Window Books
are manufactured with paper containing at least
10 percent post-consumer waste.

Library of Congress Cataloging-in-Publication Data
Donahue, Jill L. (Jill Lynn), 1967–
Way to be! : how to be brave, responsible, honest and an
all-around great kid / by Jill Lynn Donahue and Mary Small ;
illustrated by Stacey Previn.
   p. cm.–(Way to be!)
ISBN 978-1-4048-6400-9 (paperback)
1. Success in children–Juvenile literature. 2. Children–
Conduct of life–Juvenile literature. 3. Children–Life skills guides
–Juvenile literature. 4. Children–Social life and customs–
Juvenile literature. I. Small, Mary. II. Previn, Stacey. III. Title.
BF723.S77D66 2010
170.83'4–dc22   2010027022